Secret Kingdom

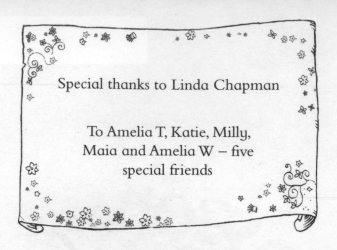

Special thanks to Linda Chapman

To Amelia T, Katie, Milly,
Maia and Amelia W – five
special friends

ORCHARD BOOKS
338 Euston Road, London NW1 3BH
Orchard Books Australia
Level 17/207 Kent Street, Sydney, NSW 2000
A Paperback Original

First published in 2012 by Orchard Books

A CIP catalogue record for this book is available
from the British Library.

ISBN 978 1 40832 038 9

1 3 5 7 9 10 8 6 4 2

Printed in Great Britain

The paper and board used in this paperback are natural recyclable
products made from wood grown in sustainable forests. The
manufacturing processes conform to the environmental regulations
of the country of origin.

Orchard Books is a division of Hachette Children's Books,
an Hachette UK company

www.hachette.co.uk

Series created by Hothouse Fiction

www.hothousefiction.com

Reading Consultant: Prue Goodwin,
lecturer in literacy and children's books

Christmas Castle

ROSIE BANKS

ORCHARD

Book
One

Contents

Christmas Eve   11

Christmas Fair   25

Queen Malice's Spell   43

A Way In!   53

The Shining Star   63

A Race to the Top!   77

Christmas Eve

"*Jingle bells, jingle bells!*" Jasmine Smith sang as she, Summer Hammond and Ellie Macdonald walked into Ellie's room.

Jasmine twirled round to grin at her two best friends, her long dark hair swinging around her. "Oh, I love Christmas Eve!"

"Me too," said Summer. "And best of all, tomorrow is Christmas Day! What presents do you two want from Santa?"

"A glitter ball for my bedroom," Jasmine said promptly. "And a music voucher."

"I'd really like some new paintbrushes," said Ellie, tucking her red curls behind her ears.

"But you've already got loads!" said Jasmine. Ellie loved art and every inch of her bedroom seemed to be crammed with paintbrushes, paints, pencils and paper.

"You can never have too many paintbrushes," smiled Ellie. She turned to Summer. "I bet you want something to do with animals."

Summer smiled. "Definitely! I saw a new book about an animal rescue centre when I was at the bookshop last week – I'd love to get that for Christmas." She sighed. "Oh, I hope Santa brings us everything we've asked for."

"We'll have to remember to leave mince pies out for him," said Jasmine. "The ones we've just put in the oven should be ready soon."

"That reminds me," Ellie said, her green eyes twinkling. "What do elves put in their mince pies?"

"What?" said Summer and Jasmine.

"*Elf*-raising flour, of course!" Ellie laughed.

Summer groaned, and Jasmine threw a cushion at Ellie.

"I wonder what the elves in the Secret Kingdom put in *their* mince pies?" Jasmine said. "I bet they make amazing mince pies at Christmas time!"

The three girls exchanged grins. No
one but them knew about the Secret
Kingdom, a magical land where all kinds
of amazing creatures lived. Summer, Ellie
and Jasmine had found out about it by
chance when they'd taken a magical box
home from their school jumble sale and
had been whisked away on an amazing
adventure! Since then they'd become the
Very Important Friends of King Merry,
the ruler of the kingdom, and helped out
whenever his horrid sister, Queen Malice,
brought trouble to the beautiful land.

"Do you think they have Christmas in
the Secret Kingdom?" wondered Summer.

"I'm sure they do," said Ellie. "It's the
most perfect place ever and Christmas is
so much fun! Shall I get the Magic Box?"

"Oh yes!" said Jasmine.

Ellie rummaged under her bed and pulled out a box about the size of a biscuit tin. Its wooden sides were carved with beautiful pictures of unicorns, mermaids and fairies, and there was a mirror on its lid surrounded by six green gems that twinkled with magic.

Summer looked at it longingly. "You know what would be the best Christmas

present ever?" she said. "Going to the
Secret Kingdom again."

Suddenly a bright golden spark flashed
across the mirrored surface of the box.

"Look!" Jasmine gasped. "The magic!
It's happening again!"

"It's a Christmas miracle!" Ellie laughed.

They all leant forward eagerly as a
string of words swirled up to the surface
of the mirrored lid. "There's a message for
us!" Jasmine said, and she read it out:

"Merry Christmas everyone,
Come and have some snowy fun!
Search for a flag and a festive show,
With holly, ivy and mistletoe."

As the last word left Jasmine's mouth,
the lid of the magic box snapped open

and red and green sparkles shot into the
air, carrying a folded piece of paper.

"The map!" Ellie
grinned. She
plucked it out
of the air and
smoothed it out
on the floor.

King Merry had
given the girls the
enchanted map on their
very first visit to the Secret Kingdom. It
was much more than an ordinary map —
it was like a window into the kingdom,
where they could see all the wonderful
places on the crescent moon-shaped
island.

Ellie spotted a coral-pink palace with
golden turrets and flags waving as if in

a slight breeze. "There's King Merry's Enchanted Palace!"

"And Glitter Beach!" said Jasmine, pointing to a strip of beautiful golden sand lapped by aquamarine waves and surrounded by tiny fairy shops and houses.

"And there's Magic Mountain!" said Summer, pointing to a snow-covered

mountain near the bottom of the island.
Pink snowflakes fell in flurries all around
it, and the girls could see snow brownies
speeding down the icy slopes on skis and
toboggans.

"But what's the answer to the riddle?"
wondered Ellie. "Where in the Secret
Kingdom are we supposed to go this
time? If it's somewhere with snow, maybe
it's Magic Mountain?"

Jasmine looked at the riddle again. "But
it says 'search for a flag', and I can't see
any flags there."

"And it says 'a festive show'," said
Summer. "I wonder what that means."

"Well, festive means Christmassy..." Ellie
murmured.

"Here!" Summer pointed at a golden
castle near King Merry's palace. Its walls

were covered with holly and ivy, it had a green-and-red flag flying from its highest tower and there was snow falling all around it. "Christmas Castle!" Summer squealed as she read the name on the map.

"It fits the riddle perfectly!" said Jasmine.

"How funny," said Ellie. "I've never even noticed it on the map before."

"Neither have I," said Summer. "But it looks so lovely and Christmassy!"

"I'm sure it's where we've got to go!" said Jasmine.

The three of them put their hands on top of the green gems on the box.

"The answer to the riddle is Christmas Castle!" Summer cried hopefully.

A loud jingle of sleigh bells rang through the air and then a ball of red and green light shot into Ellie's room. It whizzed all around the girls' heads and then burst over the bed in a shower of glittery sparkles.

A tiny pixie, sitting on a leaf, landed on Ellie's duvet. She had messy blonde hair and enormous blue eyes, and was wearing a bright red tunic trimmed with silver bells and decorated with holly leaves. "Merry Christmas!" she grinned.

"Trixibelle!" cried the girls in delight. Trixi zoomed over towards them, did a little twirl on her leaf and then stopped and hovered in the air in front of where

Ellie, Summer and Jasmine were sitting.

"Oh, it's lovely to see you all again!" she cried. "I'm so glad you got the message!"

"Is something wrong in the Secret Kingdom?" Summer asked anxiously.

"No, nothing's wrong this time," Trixi said.

The girls sighed with relief.

"King Merry just wants you to come and have some fun with us," Trixi explained. "It's Christmas Eve and we're all going to Christmas Castle to celebrate."

"I can't remember seeing Christmas Castle on the map before," said Summer.

"That's because you *haven't* seen it!" grinned Trixi. "It only appears at Christmas time! It's the most Christmassy place in the whole kingdom. There's a

huge hall where all our stockings hang
on Christmas Eve, we have an enormous
Christmas tree with a shining star on
top, and it always snows so that we have
a white Christmas. Santa brings our
presents to us there."

"So you have Santa in the Secret
Kingdom too!" said Summer in delight.

"Of course we do!" said Trixi. "Santa
goes to *every* world to deliver presents.
Anyway, King Merry sent me here today
because he was hoping you could come
and be our guests of honour at Christmas
Castle tonight. Would you like to?"

There was only one answer to that...

"Oh, yes please!" Ellie, Summmer and
Jasmine cried.

Christmas Fair

As the girls grabbed one another's hands, Trixi tapped her beautiful pixie ring and chanted:

"The celebrations have begun
So take us to the Christmas fun!"

A fountain of red, green and gold sparkles shot out of her ring and surrounded the girls in a glowing cloud. Ellie, Summer and Jasmine were whisked away, tumbling over and over in a rush of bright, beautiful colours.

Summer squeezed the others' hands
tightly as she suddenly felt them all
falling. Then she found herself landing in
something soft and tickly.

Summer opened her eyes and saw that
she, Ellie and Jasmine had fallen onto
the biggest pile of tinsel she had ever
seen! There were strands of all different
colours shimmering in the bright sunlight.
Little robins were darting around the
pile, picking up the glittering strings and
carrying them off to decorate the trees.

"Oh, wow!" gasped Jasmine, sitting
up and throwing a handful of tinsel at
Summer. "It's definitely Christmas time!"

"Everything's decorated – even you!"
Summer giggled, picking tinsel off
Jasmine's tiara.

Jasmine put her hand up to her head
and grinned as she felt the special tiara
resting there. The tiaras always appeared
on the girls' heads when they arrived in
the kingdom so that people would know
they were Very Important Friends of
King Merry's. Wearing hers always made
Jasmine feel extra-special.

"Look," Ellie said, sliding down the
mountain of tinsel to the ground and
pointing at a castle in front of them.
"We're back at the Enchanted Palace!"

The girls looked across the beautiful

palace gardens towards the coral-pink
castle where King Merry lived. There
were Christmassy stalls dotted around the
gardens, all lit by twinkly strings of fairy
lights and glittering stars. The elves who
worked in the Sugarsweet Bakery were
handing out delicious-looking mince pies
and gingerbread, and over in one corner
a band of snow brownies were playing
Christmas carols. There was a huge ice-
skating rink in front of the Enchanted
Palace, and flying reindeer were giving

sleigh rides near the lemonade fountain.

"What's going on?" Summer asked as she and Jasmine scrambled down the tinsel pile to land beside Ellie.

"It's King Merry's Christmas Fair," Trixi explained. "He always holds it here in the palace gardens on Christmas Eve."

"It's wonderful!" said Jasmine, gazing around.

"There are so many people here," said Summer excitedly.

"Everyone's invited!" said Trixi, hovering beside her on her leaf. "We have the fair here and then we all meet at the palace gates and head up to Christmas Castle. We spend Christmas Eve there, and in the morning we open our presents together."

"Like a huge Christmas sleepover," said Jasmine in delight.

"Exactly!" Trixi grinned. "And then on Christmas Day Santa comes to join us. It's so exciting!"

"Hang on!" said Ellie. "*Santa?* The real one?"

"Of course!" said a jolly voice behind them. "Didn't you know? Santa's my second cousin, twice removed. I always see him on Christmas Day, although he is usually a bit tired after delivering all the presents."

The girls turned and saw the small, plump figure of King Merry. He was wearing a bright red knitted jumper with a picture of a flying reindeer on it, and his crown was perched on top of a jaunty Santa hat. His eyes twinkled as he peered over the top of his half-moon spectacles.

"I can definitely see the family resemblance, King Merry!" Jasmine said as she hugged him. King Merry did look quite a bit like Santa, with his rosy cheeks and white beard.

King Merry chuckled happily. "Lots of people say that. Santa's taller than me, but people often think we're brothers! He's a fine chap." A look of unhappiness crossed his face. "Not like my sister."

The girls shuddered.

"Queen Malice won't come to the castle for Christmas, will she?" Summer asked anxiously, looking round as if Queen Malice or her horrible servants, the Storm Sprites, might appear on their storm clouds at any minute.

"No, my dear," King Merry said with a smile. "She is definitely not invited. Besides, Christmas is her least favourite time of year. She hates it when people are happy."

"Well, we're very glad you invited us," said Ellie. "Thank you!"

Jasmine nodded. "This is incredible!"

"The Enchanted Palace looks beautiful with all these decorations," agreed Summer. "And the fair looks like so much fun!"

The king beamed. "Oh, I am so glad you like it, girls. And just wait until you see the parade. The floats are very special indeed."

"Floats?" asked Ellie.

"Oh, yes," said King Merry excitedly. "Everyone who's staying overnight travels to Christmas Castle on a float."

A trumpeter blew a fanfare in the distance.

"There they are now!" Trixi said, grinning. "Let's go and see them!"

The girls followed King Merry and Trixi down to the palace gates. There were crowds of cheering people there and a procession of floats moved slowly past. There were all different types – a sparkling igloo with snow brownies inside, a fairy float from Glitter Beach covered in golden sand, and a huge cloud covered with weather imps – and they were all

actually floating in the air!

"This isn't like a parade back home at all!" Summer exclaimed.

"It's a million times better!" Ellie grinned.

"Look at the mermaids!" Jasmine said, pointing at a float that looked like a giant rock pool. The rocks were decorated with pink and white shells and ribbons of rainbow-coloured seaweed. Five mermaids were sitting on the rocks with their tails in the crystal-clear water, waving to the crowds as they passed.

The girls only had time to wave quickly before the mermaid float passed by them. The next float was a beautiful open glass carriage with huge silver wheels. It was being pulled by a lovely unicorn with a long silver mane and a white coat.

"It's Silvertail!" Summer called in delight.

Silvertail tossed her long mane, making her golden horn glitter in the sunlight. Her pink-maned foal, Littlehorn, pranced beside her.

"Why is Silvertail's carriage empty?" Ellie asked.

"Because it's for you!" said Trixi. "When Silvertail heard that the king had invited you girls, she asked if she could pull it herself."

Silvertail whinnied happily when she

saw the girls. "My friends from the Other
Realm!" she said as she stopped beside
them. "It's wonderful to see you again."

"It's lovely to see you both again too,"
Summer said as she stroked Littlehorn's
soft coat.

Just then a second fanfare rang out.
King Merry jumped in surprise. "The
procession's about to start," he declared.
"All aboard!" He opened the carriage
door and held out his hand to help
the girls up.

The girls felt
very important
as they took
their seats in the
carriage. There
were huge cosy
cushions to sit on

and red velvet blankets to pull over their knees.

King Merry climbed in, closed the door and settled himself in a throne opposite the girls. "Off we go!" he cried.

With Littlehorn at her side, Silvertail pranced forward and proudly followed the rest of the floats up the road. The crowd clapped and cheered and let off fireworks as each float passed by. Rainbow-coloured stars and exploding rockets lit up the sky with sparkles shaped like snowmen and holly leaves.

Jasmine and Ellie leaned out of the carriage and waved madly at everyone. Summer felt a bit shy with so many people looking at her, but after a while she got so caught up in the excitement that she forgot all about it and waved too.

"I'm so glad you could come today,"
Trixi said as she flew over and landed her
leaf on Summer's shoulder.

"Oh, me too!" sighed Summer happily.
"This is wonderful!"

"Wait until you see the castle," the pixie
smiled. "We're almost there – look!"

They turned the corner and everyone
gasped as Christmas Castle came into
view. Its golden brick walls
were covered with
thousands of tiny
fairy lights, and
it glowed like a
shining star in
the night sky.
A big green
Christmas wreath
hung on the

castle door, garlands of ivy decorated the windows and holly bushes covered with plump red berries surrounded the base. A delicious scent of cinnamon, orange and gingerbread seemed to waft out of the castle's huge chimney.

"It looks lovely," sighed Ellie.

"It is," said King Merry. "Christmas is always perfect at Christmas Castle!"

The sky darkened suddenly, and everyone looked up to see a huge black cloud rolling in front of the moon.

"Oh dear," said Trixi. "I hope there isn't a storm coming—"

CRASH!

The girls jumped as a huge clap of thunder sounded and a jagged fork of lightning shot down from the sky.

"What's going on?" said Jasmine.

The unicorns gave alarmed whinnies as four more thunderclouds appeared in the sky. On the first three clouds were thin creatures with mean faces, pointed noses and leathery wings.

"Storm Sprites!" one of the mermaids gasped.

As the last cloud appeared, everyone grew silent. On top of it stood a tall woman with a long, spiky staff and a cloud of frizzy hair. Her face was pale and her eyes were as black as pieces of coal.

"Queen Malice!" whispered Summer, her heart jumping into her throat.

"Sister!" cried King Merry.

"So you think you're going to have a wonderful Christmas, do you?" Queen Malice cackled. "Well, think again! I'll ruin Christmas for everyone!"

"Go away!" cried Jasmine bravely.

"We won't let you spoil Christmas!" yelled Ellie.

"Stupid girls!" Queen Malice hissed. "There's nothing you can do to stop me!" Eyes gleaming, she raised her black staff and pointed it straight at Christmas Castle...

Queen Malice's Spell

"Please, Sister!" cried King Merry, as he jumped out of the coach. "You mustn't ruin Christmas!"

But Queen Malice was already chanting a spell.

*"Ivy turn poisonous, holly grow tall
Surround this castle with a thorny wall!"*

A jagged green thunderbolt burst from her staff and hit the castle with a flash of light so bright that everyone blinked. When they opened their eyes they saw a dreadful sight.

Christmas Castle was almost completely covered by giant prickly holly bushes, and poison ivy was wrapped tightly around its walls. Only the very tips of the turrets and the chimney top could be seen poking out of the greenery.

Queen Malice's horrible Storm Sprites screamed with delighted laughter.

"So much for your Christmas plans, Brother!" sneered Queen Malice. "You'll never get inside for your little slumber party now! The castle will stay like this until the Shining Star glows with light – and that isn't going to happen now, is it?"

"Why you...you..." King Merry shook his fist at her.

"You're horrible!" shouted Jasmine.

"You've spoiled everything!" Trixi wailed.

"It looks like I have," Queen Malice laughed in delight. "Merry Christmas!" She clapped her hands and all the thunderclouds flew away.

For a moment everyone was too stunned to speak.

"What are we going to do now?" said Trixi with a little sob.

"Christmas is r-ruined!" stuttered King Merry.

"Wait!" Jasmine said. "We're not going to let Queen Malice get the better of us."

"No way!" said Ellie. "We've beaten her before and we'll beat her again!"

"We just need to get through the holly!" said Summer.

"Can you magic it away, Trixi?" Jasmine asked.

"I can try," Trixi said doubtfully. "But Queen Malice's spells are very powerful." She tapped her ring and called out a spell in a brave voice:

"Enchanted plants just disappear,
So we can celebrate Christmas here!"

A stream of twinkly lights scattered over
the plants. The twisted ivy and prickly
holly leaves glowed, then began to shrivel
up and shrink. But as the lights faded
away, the plants grew back just as wild
and horrible as they
were before.

"I'm sorry, my
magic's not strong
enough to break
Queen Malice's
spell," Trixi said
sadly, tears welling
up in her blue eyes.

"Don't worry," Ellie
told her. "We'll think
of something else."

"Didn't Queen Malice say
something about a star?" Summer asked.

"About the spell breaking if a star was lit?"

"Yes," said Trixi, hovering beside them on her leaf. "But it's no use. The Shining Star is a special decoration at the top of the giant Christmas tree inside the castle. Every year, I use my pixie magic to light it and start the celebrations. But I can't get into the castle to light the star, and my magic isn't strong enough to work from here."

Jasmine looked round at everyone's unhappy faces. She couldn't bear the thought of giving up. "There *must* be a way in somewhere," she said, stepping out of the carriage and walking over to the thicket of holly. She looked everywhere for an opening, but the holly was like a dense prickly wall. She tried to part the branches, but the sharp leaves caught at the skin on her hands and scratched her arms.

"Christmas is going to be a disaster!" King Merry sniffed, pulling out a handkerchief embroidered with Christmas puddings and loudly blowing his nose.

"No, it's not," said Summer, putting her arm around him. "We'll just have to go back to the Enchanted Palace and have Christmas there."

"But what about our presents?"

Littlehorn sobbed. "Santa always leaves our presents here!"

"Couldn't we get a message to him?" suggested Ellie. "Then he could come down the Enchanted Palace chimney and leave your presents there instead."

"It's too late!" wailed King Merry.

"He'll be off delivering gifts now. Our message wouldn't reach him in time."

Jasmine frowned thoughtfully. "*Down the chimney…*" she murmured to herself. Her eyes widened suddenly. "That's it!" she gasped. "I think I've got a plan!"

A Way In!

"You've thought of a way into the castle?" Ellie asked, climbing out of the carriage and walking towards Jasmine.

Jasmine nodded. "The chimney!"

"Of course!" Summer laughed as she followed Ellie out of the carriage. "If Santa can get in that way, why can't we?"

Jasmine nodded. "If Trixi goes down the chimney and lights the star, the spell will be broken, the holly will disappear and everyone else will be able to get in normally, through the door."

There was a chorus of gasps.

"Oh, you wonderful girls!" cried King Merry, jumping down from the step of the carriage. "That's a truly brilliant plan!"

"Perfect," agreed Trixi. "If I go down the chimney, I should be able to get the star lit in no time. Christmas, here we come!" She zoomed up into the night sky and headed towards the chimney.

"Uh-oh," Ellie gasped as she watched Trixi fly higher into the sky. "Look!" She pointed up at three dark shadows approaching the castle.

Summer could just make out three sets of bat-like wings as they flapped through the sky. "Storm Sprites!" she cried. "And they're heading straight for Trixi!"

"We've got to help her!" Jasmine declared.

"But how do we get up there?" Ellie asked.

"We can fly you girls up to the roof," one of the reindeer said, stepping forward. "Hop on!" He knelt down in front of Summer.

"Oh, wow!" breathed Summer as she climbed onto his back. She'd flown on a reindeer once before, at Magic Mountain, and it had been amazing. She'd always hoped she'd be able to do it again one day.

Two more reindeer knelt down so that Ellie and Jasmine could climb carefully onto their furry backs.

Ellie climbed up on hers and held on tightly. "I'm really not sure about this," she said, her heart beating fast as she looked up at the tall chimney poking out of the ivy. It was so high up! "Maybe I should stay here..."

"Don't worry," her reindeer said. "You're safe with me. My name's Starshine."

"Nice to meet you, Starshine!" Ellie said. She gave a squeal as he took off into the sky. Ellie felt a rush of fear but it only lasted for the briefest moment.

The reindeer's strides were smooth and she felt as safe as if she was sitting in an armchair.

Beside her, Summer and Jasmine whooped in delight, their hair flying out behind them as their reindeer galloped to catch up.

"We've got to get to Trixi before the Storm Sprites reach her," Summer said as they flew higher and higher towards the stars. "But I can't see her!"

"There she is!" shouted Jasmine, pointing at the castle's chimneypot. Trixi was just about to fly down into the castle.

"Trixi," Ellie called out to her. "Wait for us. And watch out for the Storm Sprites!" She looked nervously over her shoulder at the sprites, who were getting closer.

"Okay," Trixi called back, hovering over

the chimney. "But hurry!"

A moment later they reached the roof and the reindeer all landed. Their hooves sank into the prickly holly, but the thick white fur on their legs protected them.

"Thank you for the ride!" said Ellie as the girls climbed down onto the stone chimney stack.

"Good luck!" Starshine called as he and the other reindeer flew back to join their friends below. "I hope you can break the spell and let us all in!"

"Me too," called Jasmine, looking nervously over at the approaching sprites. "And soon!"

"So, how do we get down?" Ellie said, looking cautiously into the wide dark hole of the chimney. She gulped. "Do we just jump?"

"Oh, no!" Trixi said. "You might really hurt yourself if you do that. Santa uses his own special magic when he goes down chimneys. I should be able to use a spell that will help..." She frowned. "I just need to work out the words..."

"Um, Trixi," Ellie gulped, catching sight of something out of the corner of her eye. The sprites were so close now that she could see their beady eyes gleaming with mischief. "Trixi!" she gasped again. "I think you'd better come up with something quickly. The sprites are almost here!"

Trixi chanted a hasty spell:

"Girls, become light as a feather.
Float down Santa's chimney together!"

She tapped her ring and a burst of golden sparkles shot out of it and settled on the girls. "Now *jump!*" she yelled.

The girls grabbed one another's hands and leaped into the dark. They fell for a moment, and Ellie let out a squeal of fright, but then the spell began working and they started to float.

"It's so dark!" gasped Summer. It was completely black in the chimney and it was the strangest feeling to be floating downwards, not knowing where they were or when they were going to stop.

A light twinkled on and they saw Trixi
flying on her leaf. She was holding up
her ring, which was giving out a cheerful
silvery glow. "Are you all right?" she
called.

Just then the sound of shrieking high-
pitched squabbling came from above
them.

"I'm going first, Smelly Breath!"

"No, I am!"

"I am, Stinky Pants!"

"No, I am! Here I go!"

"Oh, no!" hissed Ellie. "The Storm
Sprites are coming!"

The Shining Star

Trixi tapped her pixie ring and the girls began to move faster. They shot out of the chimney and landed in a heap on a big fluffy rug beside a huge coal scuttle.

They looked up to see that they were in a massive hall with a high domed ceiling and golden walls. On every wall hung framed pictures of Santa, beaming down happily. In some he was with his reindeer, in others with lots of waving elves. Garlands of holly decked every shelf and picture. To one side of the fireplace there was a table with a large mug of hot chocolate and a massive mince pie on a plate. In the centre of the room there was an enormous Christmas tree, which was giving off a sweet smell of pine needles.

As the girls looked closer they could see that the tree was actually growing there, its roots going down into the ground

through a hole in
the castle floor.
Its topmost
branches
reached all
the way
up to the
ceiling,
and it was
decorated
with hundreds
of multi-
coloured baubles,
pine cones, candy
canes, tinsel and unlit
fairy lights. At the very top was a large,
dull star.

"That's the star we have to light!" said
Trixi, pointing at it.

The Storm Sprites' screeching voices were growing louder and louder in the chimney as they squabbled all the way down.

"I wanted to go first, Slug Brain!" one yelled.

"Well then you should have been quicker, Fungus Ears!" another replied.

"Quick, Trixi!" urged Jasmine. "You've got to light the star before the Storm Sprites get here!"

But just as Trixi began to fly up to the top of the tree on her leaf, the horrible Storm Sprites flew out of the fireplace. They faced the girls, their beady eyes gleaming.

"So, you thought you could light the Shining Star and break the spell, did you?" one of the sprites cackled. "Well, think again. We're going to stop you."

"I'd like to see you try!" cried Trixi
bravely.

She shot up into the air on her leaf.

One of the sprites grabbed a lump of
coal and threw it at her. She dodged
just in time but the other sprites quickly
joined in. Lumps of coal flew through the
air at Trixi, who had to twist and turn to
avoid them.

"Stop it!" shouted Ellie at the sprites. "Don't be so mean!"

Trixi hid behind one of the baubles on the Christmas tree.

"We told you we'd stop you, you silly little pixie!" chortled one of the sprites. "You're not going to be able to have Christmas here in the castle! You might as well give up now," he sniggered.

"Why do you have to be so horrible?" cried Jasmine, stamping her foot in exasperation. "Why do you and Queen Malice have to ruin Christmas for everyone?"

"Because we hate Christmas!" sneered the sprite. "All that silly singing and having fun."

"But what about presents?" protested Summer.

"And all the delicious food?" said Jasmine.

The sprite's eyes flickered to the mince pie on the table. "Well…" he admitted, "I suppose I *do* like presents."

"And the food *is* good," added another.

"Queen Malice *never* lets us have mince pies," grumbled the last one.

Summer's eyes widened as an idea started to form in her mind. If they could just distract the sprites for a few minutes, maybe Trixi could get up to the top of the tree. She knew the sprites were very selfish – and very greedy…

"Have you seen that mince pie over there?" she asked suddenly, pointing to the table. "It's for Santa. It looks *really* delicious but of course *you* can't have it."

"Oh, can't we?" said the sprite, putting his bony hands on his hips.

"No," said Summer. "Definitely not. It's Santa's extra-special mince pie. Just for him."

Jasmine and Ellie stared at her, wondering what she was doing. Summer winked at them.

"I would say you absolutely, most certainly *can't* have that mince pie!" Summer went on.

The sprites looked at one another and then, moving as one, they all rushed at the mince pie, pushing and elbowing the others out of the way.

"I'm having it!"

"No, I am!"

"Get off, Pointy Nose!"

"Out of my way, Dung Breath!"

As they screeched and fought, Summer raced over to the tree. "Quick, Trixi," she hissed. "Go now!"

Trixi flew up on her leaf. Ellie grabbed Summer's hands. "That was a brilliant idea," she whispered. "I hope it works."

"Come on, Trixi!" Summer breathed as she watched the pixie get closer and closer to the star. But just then one of the sprites noticed what was happening.

"What are you doing?" he shrieked at Trixi. He turned to the other sprites and yelled, "Stop her, everyone!"

The sprites leapt into the air, their leathery wings flapping.

"Watch out, Trixi!" Ellie called. "They're coming after you!"

"Quick!" cried Jasmine. "Can you use some magic?"

Trixi didn't stop to think. She hastily called out a spell:

"Pixie magic, keep those who fly
On the ground, not in the sky!"

She tapped her ring and a huge ball of light flew out of the centre of it and whizzed straight at the sprites.

As it reached them, their clouds suddenly faded away. They tried to flap their bat-like wings, but they fell to the ground in a heap.

"My cloud," the lead sprite moaned.

"My wings," called another.

"Well done, Trixi!" whooped Jasmine. "That's stopped them!"

But then something terrible happened. The ball of light turned away from the

sprites and shot back into the air.

"Oh, no!" cried Ellie as the bright light headed straight for the little pixie's leaf.

"Trixi! Watch out!"

But it was too late. The spell hit Trixi's leaf, and it suddenly plummeted downwards with her on top.

"Help!" shrieked Trixi as she tumbled through the air.

A Race to the Top!

Ellie dived forward with her hands outstretched and managed to catch Trixi just before she hit the floor.

"Oh, Ellie!" gasped Trixi, her face pale. "You saved me! Thank you!"

Ellie looked shaken too. "I'm just glad you're okay."

The sprites were groaning on the floor, trying to flap their useless wings.

"Now how are we going to get to the star?" said Summer, looking up at the star, high up at the top of the tree.

"I don't know," Trixi said. "I won't be able to fly until the spell wears off."

"We'll just have to climb," Jasmine said determinedly, running over to the tree. Summer followed close behind her.

"Wait!" Trixi called. "You need my magic to light the tree!"

Ellie helped the little pixie get safely into her pocket and ran over to the tree, trying to ignore the sick feeling in her tummy. She didn't like heights, but she had to help Trixi get to the top. "I'm not scared, I'm not scared," she muttered to herself as she grabbed the lowest branch and started to pull herself up.

"They're climbing the tree!" cried

one of the sprites
as he untangled
himself from the
pile. "Quick, get
them!"

The sprites
charged over
and started
climbing up
after the
girls. "You're
not going
to make it

to that star!" one of them hissed.

"We're going to get there first and smash
it up," another cackled.

Ellie climbed even faster. But the
sprites were gaining on her. They pulled
themselves up the tree, their bony fingers

grasping the prickly branches.

One sprite raced past Ellie, bumping her with his bat-like wing as he passed. Soon he was level with Summer. "We're going to beat you!" he crowed.

"Oh, really?" cried Jasmine. She grabbed a piece of tinsel off the tree and threw it at him as he reached the branch below her. The tinsel fell over the sprite's eyes, and he stopped to pull it off.

"Yuck!" he spat. "Sparkly stuff!"

Meanwhile, Summer was throwing all the pine cones and candy canes she could reach at the other two sprites. "Stop it!" they shrieked, ducking behind the branches as the ornaments rained down on them.

"It's up to you, Ellie!" Jasmine cried. "We'll hold them off. You've got to get Trixi to the star!"

Gritting her teeth, Ellie pulled herself up the tree as fast as she could.

"I can see the star!" Trixi called, peeping out of Ellie's pocket. "We're almost there!"

Ellie could feel the tree shaking below her and hear the sprites' shrieks and cries as she climbed higher and higher. But there was no time to look around. She pulled herself up onto another branch, and another, until finally she was at the

very top of the tree.
Shakily, she let go
with one hand,
and helped Trixi
out of her pocket.
Then she held the
little pixie up as
high as she could. Trixi stood
on tiptoe on Ellie's hand and stretched up
to the star.

"NO!" screeched the sprites, seeing
what was happening.

But it was too late. Trixi tapped her ring
against the star and gasped out:

"Shining Star, light up bright,
Bring joy and laughter here tonight!"

A shower of golden sparks rushed out

of the centre of her ring and swirled in a
whirlwind around the star. The Shining
Star began to glow, faintly at first, but
brighter and brighter with every second,

until its sparkling light lit up the room.
There was a BANG like the loudest
Christmas cracker in the world as the
poison ivy winding around the castle

exploded into a shower of green sparks.
The holly bushes outside the windows
began to shrink back down to normal,
their branches writhing like snakes as they
got smaller and smaller.

"Yippee!" cried Trixi as all the fairy
lights on the tree suddenly burst into
sparkling light. "Queen Malice's spell is
broken!"

Howling in disappointment, the sprites
scrambled back down the tree.

"You don't have to go, Storm Sprites!"
called Jasmine with a grin. "I'm sure King
Merry would give you a mince pie and
let you stay. There'll be lots of singing and
dancing."

"And tinsel," added Summer.

"Gah!" cried the sprites as they ran
angrily to the door.

"Queen Malice will hear about this!"
one cried as he pulled the door open,
almost knocking
King Merry
flying as he
ran past.

"Oh my
goodness!"
King Merry
exclaimed,
staggering back
in surprise.

Summer and Jasmine grinned at each
other and climbed down the tree.

"You did it!" King Merry cried. "Oh,
girls! You saved Christmas for us all!"

"It was Trixi and Ellie, really!" Jasmine
said, pointing to where Ellie was still
clinging to the top of the Christmas tree.

"I'll get them," laughed Starshine, galloping up into the air. Seconds later he returned with Ellie safely on his back.

"You were so brave!" Summer told Ellie as she helped her down and gave her a big hug.

"Look!" cried Trixi as her leaf swirled off the floor and swooped over to her. She jumped onto it and whizzed around the girls' heads. "My flying magic's back!"

King Merry did a little jig of happiness on the spot. "The star is shining and the poison ivy's gone. Now our Christmas Eve celebrations can really begin!"

Everyone cheered. A group of tiny fairies flew around the room waving their wands and putting up even more fairy lights to make the room extra sparkly. The unicorns, reindeer, elves, pixies, brownies and imps all crowded inside the castle, and the mermaids' rock-pool float came in completely so the mermaids could still be part of the fun.

The mermaids started singing a Christmas carol, and soon the hall was ringing with the merry music. The girls joined in as best they could. They knew all the tunes, but the words were rather different!

"Imagine if we went back to school and sang '*Frosty the Snow Brownie*' and '*Hark the Herald Mermaids Sing*'," grinned Ellie. "We'd get some very strange looks."

"Or '*Jingle Elves*'," said Jasmine. "Can you imagine what Mrs Benson would say?"

They all giggled at the thought of their teacher hearing the Secret Kingdom versions of the carols.

"Oh, this is so much fun!" said Summer as the singing stopped and the elves started handing out food and drinks. She grinned as an elf handed her a mug of hot chocolate with marshmallows, sugar stars and cream decorating the top. "I've had the best evening ever."

"It hasn't finished yet," said Trixi. "It's time to put our stockings up now!"

Everyone watched as the little pixie flew to the fireplace and tapped her ring.

"A stocking for everyone,
hanging just right
For Santa to fill when he
comes here tonight,"

she called in her tinkly voice.

Red light flashed through the air and golden sparks exploded from Trixi's pixie ring. Suddenly the fireplace was hung with a mass of brightly coloured stockings, each with its owner's name embroidered on the front. Right in the centre of the mantelpiece was one particularly big purple stocking with gold crowns on it and "King Merry" embroidered in gold thread.

"Oh, wow!" breathed Summer.

"I really wish we could stay here overnight," said Jasmine longingly. "I'd love to be here in the morning."

"I know, but we should go home," said Ellie. "Santa will be bringing our presents to our world – and I would like to see Mum, Dad and Molly. It's lovely being here, but I want to spend Christmas with them as well."

Summer and Jasmine nodded. They knew exactly how she felt.

"Thank you so much for inviting us here for Christmas Eve," Jasmine said to Trixi and King Merry. "I just wish we could see you all on Christmas Day too."

"Well, that's a wish that's easily granted," King Merry chuckled. "Why don't you come back in the morning?"

"Can we really?" asked Summer.

King Merry nodded. "Of course!"

"Look for a message in the Magic Box at eleven o'clock," said Trixi.

The girls exchanged delighted looks. "So we'll get to have two Christmases!" said Ellie. "One at home – and one with all our friends here!"

"Exactly!" King Merry hugged them all. "Now, have a lovely Christmas Eve back in your world and we'll see you tomorrow!"

"Merry Christmas, everyone!" Ellie, Summer and Jasmine called as Trixi tapped her pixie ring and a swirl of gold and red sparks whisked them away.

The girls landed back on the floor in Ellie's bedroom with a bump. Ellie blinked. "We're home again!" She glanced at her bedside clock and saw that, as usual, no time at all had passed since they had gone.

"It feels strange to be back," said Jasmine, looking round the room. "It's only afternoon here, but in the Secret Kingdom everyone is going to bed!"

Ellie looked at the Magic Box and smiled. It might have stopped glowing now, but she knew that the very next day they'd be going back to the Secret Kingdom again!

"We should go home and put our own stockings out," said Summer. "And tomorrow morning, we can all meet at my house just before eleven. Then we can go to the Secret Kingdom for a magical Christmas!"

Ellie grinned. "You know, I think I want to go to bed right now so the morning comes as quickly as possible!"

"You can't go to bed just yet," said Jasmine. "There are mince pies cooking."

"And they smell almost as delicious as the ones in the Secret Kingdom," said Summer, sniffing the air.

"It's lucky there aren't any Storm Sprites around!" chuckled Ellie.

Giggling together, the three girls ran downstairs. One adventure might be over, but another was still to come!

Book Two

Contents

Christmas Morning   99

Back to the Secret Kingdom   111

Santa's Sleigh   125

Sleigh Chase   139

Searching High and Low   149

Magic Spells   163

Christmas Magic   179

Christmas Morning

"CRASH!" cried Finn, Summer's three-year-old brother, as he bashed his new train through a pile of wrapping paper.

Connor, who was two years older than Finn, roared and ran round the room in his new dragon costume. "I'm coming to get you, Summer!" he shouted.

"No!" Summer cried, pretending to be scared as Connor dived on top of her. "Please, no!" She tickled him until he squealed and wriggled away, nearly knocking over the Christmas tree with all its decorations as he went.

"I love Christmas and I love Santa!" he declared.

"Me too," said Summer happily, touching the new dolphin necklace that she'd found in her stocking that morning. The pendant was made out of sparkling blue glass and the chain was silver. She couldn't wait to show it to Ellie and Jasmine.

Excitement fizzed through her. Not just because it was Christmas Day and she was going to see her two best friends soon, but also because the three of them were going to a special Christmas celebration in the Secret Kingdom. All of their magical friends would be there – along with King Merry's cousin, Santa!

Summer wished she could take her brothers with her, but she knew that she,

Ellie and Jasmine couldn't tell anyone about the Secret Kingdom.

The doorbell rang. Summer raced to the front door and threw it open. Ellie and Jasmine were standing in the snow outside.

"Merry Christmas!" exclaimed Ellie, flinging her arms around Summer. Her green eyes were shining and snowflakes decorated her red curls.

Jasmine was wearing a hat with brown reindeer antlers on it and a bright pink scarf.

"I like the look, Jasmine!" grinned Summer.

Jasmine danced into the house in her polka-dot wellies. "I think it's rather cool, myself! Happy Christmas! What did Santa bring you?"

"This!" Summer held up the necklace.

"It's gorgeous!" Ellie grinned. "I got a brand-new paint set with lots of different types of paints. It was just what I wanted."

"I got a glitter ball and this reindeer hat," said Jasmine as she took off her hat and coat.

"Hey, I've got a joke!" said Ellie with a grin. "What do reindeer hang on their Christmas trees?"

"What?" said Summer.

"Horn-aments!" Ellie giggled.

Summer and Jasmine groaned.

"If you think that's bad, then listen to this one—" Ellie began.

"Hang on!" interrupted Summer, glancing at the clock and seeing that there were only a couple of minutes until eleven o'clock. "Let's go upstairs now and get out the…" she lowered her voice, "you-know-what."

As Summer spoke, her mum came through from the kitchen with Mike, Summer's step-dad. "Merry Christmas, girls!" Mrs Hammond said. "It's lovely to see you."

"Brrr!" said Mike, rubbing his arms. "It's very snowy out there. Would you like a mince pie to warm you up?"

"Thanks, but maybe in a minute," Jasmine said quickly, glancing at Ellie and Summer, who both nodded. None of them wanted to miss getting the special Christmas message in the Magic Box.

"Can I show Ellie and Jasmine some of the presents in my room first?" Summer asked.

"Sure," Mike said with a smile. "Off you go!"

Summer, Ellie and Jasmine raced upstairs and into Summer's bedroom, which was warm and cheerful. The room was painted a sunny yellow and there were animal posters on all the walls. Summer had hung a bird feeder outside her window, and two robins were perched on the windowsill, pecking at the birdseed. In one corner Summer had put up a small artificial Christmas tree with flashing lights and pretty tinsel all over it.

A golden angel was perched at the top.

"You're so lucky to have your own tree," said Jasmine. "It looks really beautiful."

"Mum said I could have it when Finn and Connor started covering the big tree downstairs with monster truck decorations they'd made." Summer giggled.

"And there's the Magic Box!" said Ellie, spotting the wooden box nestled under the tree.

"I can't believe we're actually going to meet the real Santa today!" Summer said excitedly as she pulled  the box out from under the tree.

Jasmine sighed happily. "Oh, this is going to be the best Christmas ever!"

"Look, the message!" Ellie gasped as the Magic Box started to glow.

The three girls leaned forward eagerly as a riddle appeared in the mirrored lid of the box. Summer read it out loud:

"Where there's a tree
and a bright shining star,
That's where the Christmas fun
and games are!"

"Well, that's easy," said Jasmine. "I don't think we even need to look at the map this time."

"There's only one place it could be," said Ellie. She looked at the others expectantly. They all put their hands on the green gems that studded the box.

"Christmas Castle!" they chorused.

There was the sound of sleigh bells jingling and then a golden ball of light whizzed around the room. The light hit Summer's Christmas tree and suddenly Trixi was there among the branches, sitting on her leaf. Today she was wearing a green tunic embroidered with silver snowflakes, and her messy blonde hair was hidden under a Santa hat. She had fluffy red boots on her feet and a golden belt around her waist.

"Trixi!" Jasmine said delightedly. "You're here!"

"Now we can go to the Secret Kingdom," said Ellie excitedly.

"Wait!" Summer put a hand on both her friends' arms. "Trixi, are you okay?" she asked. The little pixie didn't have her usual beaming smile. Her face was pale

and her blue eyes were brimming with
tears. Summer kneeled down and gently
held out her hand. Trixi stepped off her
leaf onto Summer's hand and gave a sob.

Jasmine and Ellie crowded around.
"What's happened, Trixi?" asked Jasmine
anxiously.

"It's…it's Santa!" wept Trixi.

"What about him?" asked Ellie.

Trixi raised her tear-stained face. "He…
he hasn't come to Christmas Castle.
When we woke up this morning, all our
stockings were empty!"

Back to the Secret Kingdom

"Santa hasn't come to Christmas Castle!" Ellie echoed in shock.

"No," Trixi sniffed. "He went around the rest of the kingdom, but he didn't come to the castle."

"That's dreadful!" exclaimed Jasmine.

"Please will you come to Christmas Castle with me and see if you can help?" begged Trixi. "Everyone's so upset."

"Of course we'll come," said Summer.

Trixi's little shoulders sagged in relief. "Thank you so much!" She tapped the pixie ring on her finger and spoke shakily:

"To Christmas Castle we must go,
Take us there through rain or snow."

Summer, Ellie and Jasmine held hands as green and gold snowflakes shot out of Trixi's pixie ring and whirled around them. The girls spun away in the whirlwind, twirling round in the air until they felt their feet touch down on a soft rug.

Ellie breathed in the wintry scent of pine needles. She opened her eyes and saw that the special tiaras that showed everyone in the Secret Kingdom that she,

Summer and Jasmine were King Merry's special helpers had magically appeared on their heads. She looked around to see that she and her two friends were standing beside the enormous tree in Christmas Castle's great hall. It grew up through a hole in the floor and its highest branches were just touching the ceiling beams far above them.

The fairy lights strung around the tree were shining brightly and the star sparkled on the top just as it had done the night before, but apart from the tree, things were very different at the castle. The elves, brownies and pixies were all crying. The fairies fluttering overhead were talking sadly to one another. The unicorns' heads were drooping miserably. King Merry was sitting in an armchair, blowing his nose noisily on a large handkerchief embroidered with Christmas puddings, his red Santa hat drooping down underneath his crown. "Oh, dearie me," he was murmuring to himself. "Dearie, dearie me."

"King Merry!" said Summer, hurrying forward and kneeling beside him. "We've just heard what happened."

"Oh, girls, I'm so glad you're here!" exclaimed King Merry, taking Summer's hand. "Santa didn't come!" He looked at all the empty stockings hanging on the fireplace and shook his head sadly. "He must have forgotten us."

"Santa wouldn't forget!" said Summer. "Something must have happened to him."

Jasmine frowned. "Or someone," she said. "I bet Queen Malice has something to do with this."

"No!" spluttered King Merry. "Even my sister wouldn't stop Santa from delivering presents!" He looked round at everyone's unhappy faces and then groaned. "Oh, of course she would! It's just the sort of thing she would do."

Ellie looked round. "I wonder if there are any clues about what's happened," she said.

Jasmine walked over to the fireplace and looked at it thoughtfully. "If Santa was here, he'd have come down the chimney..." she murmured to herself. Just then she saw something small and round shining on the floor behind the coal scuttle. She swooped down and picked it up. It was a gold button with a picture of holly leaves on it. "Look!" she cried.

"Gracious me!" King Merry exclaimed. "That belongs to Santa. It's one of the buttons from his coat. But how did it get there?"

"Santa must have been here after all," Summer cried. "See, he didn't forget you!"

"Look!" Ellie gasped, pointing to the soot in the fireplace, which was moving as if it was alive. As they watched, the black dust started to swirl around and form letters in the fireplace. Suddenly the chimney echoed with a familiar cackling laugh.

"It's a message from Queen Malice!" Summer said in horror.

Jasmine read it out loud:

"You thought you'd won
and saved the day,
But I captured Santa when
he left his sleigh.
There'll be no Christmas
presents for you,
And there's nothing you can do!"

There was a chorus
of gasps and cries.
"Queen Malice
has kidnapped
Santa!"
whispered Trixi.
"Oh, no!"
wailed King
Merry.

"Don't worry," said Summer, putting her arm around a crying brownie. "We'll rescue him."

Just then a strange snorting noise echoed down the chimney.

"Queen Malice!" said one of the unicorns in fright.

"It doesn't sound like Queen Malice," said Jasmine thoughtfully.

The noise came again. There was a snort and the stomp of hooves.

Summer frowned. "It sounds like an animal, but what animal would be on the roof?"

"Santa's reindeer, of course!" gasped Ellie.

"Oh, yes!" exclaimed King Merry. "Santa always leaves his sleigh up there when he comes down the chimney."

"Maybe they can tell us what has happened," said Jasmine. She turned to Trixi. "Can you use your magic to take us up there so we can ask them?" she asked.

"Of course!" Trixi said. She whizzed down on her leaf until it was hovering by the fireplace and then she tapped her ring and chanted:

"Magic leaf, grow tall and wide,
Enough to give my friends a ride!"

Green sparkles flew out of the ring and hit the leaf. For a moment the whole thing seemed to shine, and then it started to grow. Ellie, Summer and Jasmine leapt back as they were almost knocked over by the rapidly growing leaf. When it finally stopped, it hovered in the air like a magic carpet.

"I'm coming too, Trixi!" said King Merry.

"Jump on board!" cried Trixi, patting the glowing leaf. "There's enough room for everyone. It'll take us up to the roof."

"It's a good thing the chimney here at Christmas Castle is so huge," said Summer as she stepped up. "Otherwise we'd never fit!"

Ellie climbed up onto the hovering leaf
and gulped. She didn't like heights, and
the idea of riding so high into the air
made her nervous. Summer and Jasmine
saw her face and grabbed her hands.

"Come on!" Jasmine said to her. "You'll
be fine."

The leaf
bounced
slightly in
the air as
they sat
down.

"Don't
worry, Ellie,"
said Trixi reassuringly.
"My magic will keep you safe. I promise
you won't fall off." She raised her ring in
the air. "Are you ready?"

The girls and King Merry all nodded.

"Then up the chimney we go!" Trixi called, tapping her ring.

Santa's Sleigh

"Oh, wow!" gasped Jasmine as the leaf rose up the chimney. "This feels weird. It's like being in a magical lift!"

Ellie shut her eyes tightly.

Summer peered above them. She could see a patch of light getting closer and closer. "I can see the top of the chimney!" she cried excitedly.

The leaf climbed higher and higher and then burst out into the sky.

"Yippee!" yelled King Merry.

Ellie felt the cold air sting their cheeks, and opened her eyes. She immediately wished she hadn't. They were floating above the castle roof, and the castle grounds were spread out far beneath them.

"Look!" Jasmine exclaimed as she gazed down at the snowy gardens, holly bushes and a courtyard with a giant snowman and a barn.

"Wow!" Summer gasped. Directly below them on the roof was a big glossy red sleigh led by nine reindeer. "That must be Santa's sleigh – and it's full of presents!" At the back of the sleigh was a huge sack bulging with presents wrapped in beautiful Christmassy paper, tied with huge ribbon bows.

Trixi tapped her ring and the leaf floated down to the roof, landing on the tiles beside the sleigh before shrinking back to its usual size.

King Merry and the girls clambered over the roof tiles to the reindeer. Their leather harness was hung with silver bells that tinkled when they moved, and magic seemed to sparkle off every hair on their bodies.

"Hello," one of the reindeer snorted. "Hello," Summer said shyly as the reindeer snuffled at her palm. The deer had soft, brown eyes with long eyelashes, and white spots on her coat. "You're Dancer!" Summer said excitedly, reading out the name written on the reindeer's harness in gold letters.

"And I'm Dasher," said the reindeer next to her, who was slightly larger. His coat was a beautiful chestnut-brown colour, and he had large velvety antlers. He spotted the girls' tiaras. "You must be the visitors from the Other Realm!" he said, looking awestruck. "We've heard so much about you!"

"And we've heard so much about you!" Summer smiled, hardly able to believe that Santa's reindeer had heard about her. "I'm Summer and this is Jasmine and Ellie," she said, pointing to each of her friends in turn.

Dancer pawed at the tiles as the snow fell more heavily. "Have you seen Santa?" she asked anxiously. "He left us here ages ago. We always finish the Secret Kingdom present delivery here at Christmas Castle. Santa usually goes down the chimney to deliver the presents and then comes back up and takes us to the barn where we can have a rest before we fly home to the North Pole."

"But as we got here we heard a strange noise from the chimney," said Dasher. "Santa went to investigate it and he hasn't come back. Do you know where he is?"

The girls exchanged worried looks.

"We don't know where he is exactly," admitted Jasmine sadly. "But, well, we do know that the queen has kidnapped him."

"Queen Malice!" the reindeer snorted
in alarm.

"But he can't be far away!" a voice
said. A reindeer at the very front of the
sleigh turned to face them and the girls
saw that his red nose was glowing softly.

"Rudolph!" exclaimed Jasmine, her eyes
wide.

Rudolph nodded.
"My nose
always glows
when I'm
near Santa."

"But it's
glowing
now,"
Jasmine
said in
confusion.

"So Santa must be nearby!" Ellie gasped.

All the other reindeer whinnied in relief.

"If Queen Malice had taken Santa away from here," Rudolph said shyly, "then my nose wouldn't be shining now. Which means he must be somewhere here at Christmas Castle."

"Then we should get looking," said Jasmine determinedly.

"Climb into the sleigh," said Dancer. "We'll fly you back down."

King Merry started towards the sleigh, but as he did, Summer heard a strange noise. "What was that?" she asked, peering into the sleigh. It sounded like it was coming from Santa's sack. Suddenly she heard it again. "It sounds like the rustle of wrapping paper…" she said excitedly. "Maybe it's Santa!"

"Santa?" called Jasmine warily.

There was a low sniggering laugh.

"SURPRISE!" shrieked a chorus of
cackling voices. Wrapping paper flew up
into the air and five Storm Sprites leapt
out from under the sack of presents.

Everyone gasped,
and King Merry
fell over onto his
bottom.

The reindeer
strained to
look back at
the sleigh, but
they couldn't
turn far enough
in their harness to
see what was happening
behind them. "What's going on?" Dancer
called.

"Queen Malice's Storm Sprites have
sneaked into the sleigh!" Jasmine told
them.

"And we've got all your presents,"
gloated one of the sprites. He held up a

long rainbow-coloured scarf. "Lovely!" he
cackled as he wrapped it round his neck.

"Look at my pretty dress!" gloated a
second sprite, holding
up a tiny dress
embroidered with
holly.

"That's the
dress I asked
Santa for!"
stammered
Trixi, her eyes
wide.

A third sprite
pulled out a
pair of fluffy purple
slippers with golden crowns
on them. He put them on his feet and
wiggled his spiky toes.

"Those are the slippers I was hoping to get!" spluttered King Merry. "Oh, you horrible creature!" he exclaimed as the sprite danced around the sleigh wearing the slippers.

"Those aren't your presents," Jasmine shouted. "Give them back!"

"Shan't!" taunted the sprites. Cackling in delight, they grabbed the sack and heaved it up into the air.

"They're taking the presents!" gasped Jasmine as the sprites flew up into the sky, pulling the sack along with them. "We've got to stop them!"

Sleigh Chase

"Jump into the sleigh!" Dancer called.

The girls quickly climbed onto the
driver's seat. They pulled a snuggly rug
over their legs and cuddled up as the
snow started to fall more heavily. The
Storm Sprites were already so far ahead
that they looked like dark specks in the
snowy sky.

Trixi helped King Merry clamber
inside the sleigh, then swooped down and
landed neatly on the driver's seat between
Summer and Ellie.

"Follow those sprites!" Ellie called to the reindeer. "Full speed ahead!"

"Here we go!" called Dancer.

She and the other reindeer took off from the high castle roof, with Rudolph and his red nose leading the way. Golden sparks flew from their hooves as they rose into the sky. Even though they were going fast, Ellie felt safe in the sleigh. She, Jasmine and Summer laughed in delight as they flew through the swirling snowflakes, sparks shooting up around them like a firework display.

"Isn't this amazing?" Summer gasped as the wind blew her hair back from her face. "We're riding in Santa's sleigh!"

"And we're catching up!" Jasmine whooped. She pointed in front of them, where the Storm Sprites were struggling

to fly and hold onto Santa's sack at the
same time. Their bat-like wings were
flapping frantically as they wobbled
through the air.

"Give us the sack back, you horrid
things!" called Ellie.

"NO!" shrieked the sprites.

"How are we going to get the sack
from them?" asked Jasmine. "I don't think
we can get close enough to them in the
sleigh to grab it."

"Is there anything you can do, Trixi?" Summer asked.

Trixi thought for a minute, then tapped her pixie ring and chanted:

*"Give us some freezing things to throw,
To stop those sprites with ice and snow!"*

A flurry of
silver sparkles
flew from
Trixi's ring,
and instantly
everyone's
hands were

filled with snowballs.

The girls and King Merry started to throw the frozen balls at the sprites.

"Take that!" Jasmine called as she

launched a snowball at the lead sprite.

"Ouch!" he squealed as it hit the back
of his head.

Suddenly, as the sprites ducked and
dived to avoid the snowballs, the sack
slipped out of their hands and plummeted
down towards the ground, spilling
presents as it went.

"Hold on tight!" Rudolph
called. "We'll get it!"

He led the other reindeer
in a steep dive. Just before
the sack hit the ground,
the sleigh swooped
beneath it, and the
sack and all the
presents landed in the
back with a thud. With
a tinkle of sleigh bells, the

reindeer soared back up high into the sky.

"Argh!" yelled one of the sprites.

"The presents!" another yelped. "Let's get out of here before Queen Malice finds out we've lost them!"

The sprites flew away, howling and yelling as they went.

"Phew!" said Summer. "They've gone!"

"And we've got the presents!" said Ellie gleefully.

Summer peered into the sack and frowned. "But they don't seem to have labels on them," she said. "We still can't give them out – only Santa knows who they're for."

"Then we'll just have to find Santa," Ellie grinned.

"We're almost down!" cried Jasmine, looking over the side of the sleigh.

The girls held hands as the reindeer landed the sleigh in the snowy courtyard next to a snowman. There wasn't even the slightest bump – they touched down as lightly as a feather.

"Thank you," Ellie said to the reindeer as she and the others jumped out.

The snow was almost like a blizzard now. Summer smiled as she saw Rudolph's nose glowing through it. It looked even brighter now in the swirling snow. "I can see why Santa chose you to lead the sleigh," she told him, stroking his velvety back.

"We'd better take Santa's sack into Christmas Castle," Jasmine said to the reindeer. "Then we can get everyone to help us look for Santa."

"But what about you?" Summer asked

the reindeer. "You must be really tired now after such a long night."

"We can wait in the barn," said Rudolph. "It's always very cosy in there."

Summer ran through the snow to open the barn door. The reindeer all trotted inside gratefully, pulling the sleigh behind them. There was a deep bed of warm straw and a manger full of sweet-smelling hay all ready for them. Trixi tapped her ring and magically undid their harnesses,

and the reindeer stepped out of them gratefully.

"Thank you, everyone," snorted Rudolph. "I hope you find Santa soon."

Summer frowned. For some reason he looked different from a moment ago. She stared at him, but she couldn't work out what had changed.

"Come on, Summer!" called Ellie from the castle doorway.

Summer pushed thoughts of Rudolph from her mind. "See you later," she promised. "We'll come and tell you just as soon as we find Santa!"

Searching High and Low

"So everyone knows where they're going to look?" Jasmine checked. She was standing on a chair in the great hall addressing everyone. "And you all know which group you are searching with?"

The pixies, elves, brownies, imps and unicorns in front of her nodded eagerly. The girls had split them into groups and each group was going to search a different part of the castle.

"We will find Santa!" King Merry
declared. "We'll search high and low!"

Everyone cheered and the unicorns
whinnied and stamped their hooves.

Jasmine jumped down from the chair.
"Right," she said, getting in her group
with Ellie, Summer, King Merry, Trixi
and two snow brownies called Hailstone
and Icy. "We're checking the top floor of
the castle."

There were a lot of stairs in the castle
and although the girls and the brownies
ran up them easily, King Merry huffed
and wheezed as he made his way slowly
up. By the time he reached the second
flight he had to stop for breath. "Oh,
dearie me," he puffed, fanning his face
with his handkerchief. "I'm not as fit as
I used to be. Maybe you young things

should go on without me."

"I'll give you a hand, King Merry!"
Trixi said. She tapped her ring and silver
wings sprouted on the backs of the king's
shoes.

"Whoa!" King Merry
gasped, his arms
windmilling as
his shoes lifted
him into
the air and
started
carrying
him
up the
stairs. "Oh,
holly and
mistletoe!" he
added. "That's better!"

The girls grinned and raced after him, with the brownies following. They reached the top floor and looked down a long corridor with lots of bedroom doors on either side.

Ellie opened the first door. The room was covered in beautiful wall hangings embroidered with magical robins that actually hopped from branch to branch. "Wow!" she breathed, stepping inside.

The smell of pine needles hung in the

air and fairy lights decorated the ceiling.
There was a big four-poster bed, and a
glass bowl of chocolates and candy canes
sat on the dressing table beside it. Ellie
looked in the wardrobe while Summer
checked behind the curtains and Jasmine
looked under the bed, but there was no
sign of Santa.

"He's not in here," said Jasmine at last.
"Let's try the next room."

They worked their way along the
landing, opening door after door on the
right-hand side. The brownies searched
the rooms on the left side of the landing,
while King Merry tried to slow the wings
on his shoes down and zoomed up and
down past the bedroom
doors. There
were enough
bedrooms
for all the
guests
from the
Secret
Kingdom
to stay over
on Christmas Eve,
and each one was more
Christmassy than the last.

"That was the final room on this floor," said Jasmine sadly as she shut a door at the end of the landing. "He's not here."

"Don't worry," Summer comforted her. "Maybe one of the other groups has found him."

The group headed back downstairs into the great hall. Santa's sack full of presents was there sitting under the tree, but the room didn't seem Christmassy at all. The rest of the guests at the castle were standing around, looking sad.

"Oh dear," said Summer, seeing the anxious looks on everyone's faces. "It doesn't look like they have found Santa."

Jasmine went over to talk to the other groups and find out if anyone had seen Santa.

"Every inch of Christmas Castle has

been searched, and no one's found him," she told the others glumly as she came back over them. "Santa isn't here after all."

"Rudolph must have got it wrong," said Ellie.

"Let's go and talk to him," said Summer. "Maybe he can help somehow."

The girls and Trixi went back out to the barn. The reindeer all crowded round as the girls opened the door.

"Have you found Santa?" Dancer asked eagerly.

"No," Ellie sighed, patting her soft coat. "And we've looked everywhere."

"Are you absolutely sure your nose only glows when you're near him, Rudolph?" Jasmine asked.

Rudolph nodded. "Definitely."

Summer looked at
Rudolph's nose.
It was still
glowing, but
only a little
bit. She
frowned.
She'd been
sure his
nose had
been glowing
much more
brightly when they'd
landed in the blizzard. "Does your nose
glow more when it's snowing?" she asked
him suddenly.

Rudolph looked surprised. "No, it only
glows brightly when I'm near Santa."

Summer thought for a minute.

"Rudolph, will you come outside with me?" she asked. "It will only take a minute. I just want to check something."

"Sure," he said, following her outside into the courtyard.

"Your nose!" Summer exclaimed.

"What?" Rudolph said anxiously, crossing his eyes as he tried to look at it.

"It's shining more brightly," said Trixi, flying up to Rudolph's nose on her leaf.

"It's getting brighter and brighter," said Jasmine as Rudolph walked further into the courtyard. "We must be nearer to Santa here than we were in the barn!"

"We can follow your nose to Santa!" Ellie grinned.

"Of course!" Rudolph said, looking excited. He started trotting through the snow towards the castle door, but suddenly Summer stopped him.

"Wait!" she cried. "Your nose is glowing less now. Santa can't be that way."

"So, where is he then?" said Ellie, looking around the snowy courtyard. "Is he out in the garden?"

Rudolph came back towards where they were standing, his nose glowing brighter and brighter as he walked. By the time he was standing next to Summer, his nose was sparkling and glittering as brightly as a star.

"Santa must be somewhere near here!" Summer cried. She looked all around, but the only thing she could see nearby was the snowman. She hadn't noticed it properly before, but now she really looked at it. It was a life-sized Santa made out of snow. It really was very realistic. The snow had been shaped to look like the fur on Santa's trousers and hat, and there were even

little snowy buttons on the coat. Suddenly Summer gasped. "Ellie! Jasmine! Trixi! Rudolph!" she cried excitedly. "I think I know where Santa is!"

Magic Spells

Summer pointed at the snow Santa.
"I think Santa's been turned into a
snowman by Queen Malice!"

Rudolph walked around the snowman,
studying it closely. "It does look like
Santa," he said, his eyes wide. "His beard
is exactly that long and curly…"

"And look!" Summer cried. "He's missing a button on his jacket!"

"It must be him then!" said Jasmine, pulling the button that she'd found by the fireplace earlier out of her pocket. Sure enough, it matched the other buttons perfectly – except that it was made of gold instead of snow.

"But how do we get him out of there?" Ellie asked.

"I'll try and break the spell," said Trixi. She thought for a moment and then tapped her ring and chanted:

"Snow and ice please melt away,
Free Santa now to save the day!"

Golden sparkles flew out of the ring and surrounded the snow Santa. The girls held their breath, but nothing happened.

Trixi's shoulders sagged. "I'm sorry," she said sadly. "It doesn't look like my magic's strong enough to break the spell."

"I know!" said Ellie suddenly. "What about the snow brownies? They can do special magic with snow and ice, can't they?"

"They could at Magic Mountain," Jasmine said, remembering their visit to the snowy wonderland. "Maybe they can help."

The girls looked at one another, hope lighting up their eyes.

"Let's go and get them!" cried Summer.

"So this is really Santa?" King Merry asked.

Everyone who had been in the hall was now outside, clustered around the snow Santa.

"We think so," said Summer.

"We were hoping the snow brownies might be able to help break the spell," said Ellie.

Hailstone looked at the snow Santa thoughtfully. "We'll try," he said. "But to work snow magic this powerful we'll need some help."

"Everyone make a big circle," Icy called, "and hold hands."

The elves, pixies and imps all formed
a circle and joined hands with the girls
and King Merry. When everyone was in
place, Hailstone began to chant:

"Cold snow melt and frozen ice crack.
Brownie magic, bring Santa back!"

Summer felt a warm tingle in her
hands. The elf next to her gasped and
Summer was sure she'd felt it too.

Icy joined in with Hailstone's chant, repeating the words. The warmth increased. Suddenly Summer didn't feel cold at all. Her whole body felt as if it was glowing.

"All together!" cried Hailstone.

And everyone chanted together:

*"Cold snow melt and frozen ice crack.
Brownie magic, bring Santa BACK!"*

Suddenly, the snow Santa's suit started to glow a faint red colour.

"It's working!" Jasmine gasped.

There was a cracking noise and the smooth surface of the snow Santa splintered into hundreds of tiny cracks. The red light grew stronger and stronger as the snow and ice melted away.

Finally the last of the snow fell from the top of the snow Santa's head. When the snow finally settled, everyone gasped. Santa Claus himself was standing there in the middle of the courtyard! "Ho, ho, HELP!" he cried. Then he saw everyone in front of him and let out a deep belly laugh. "My Secret Kingdom friends!" he boomed. "I'm so glad to see you! The last thing I remember was hearing a horrible cackling laugh from inside Christmas Castle. I went down the chimney to investigate, and that horrid Queen Malice appeared. Before I could do anything to stop her, she cast a horrible spell on me."

"Cousin!" King Merry cried, running forwards and hugging Santa. "Oh, it's good to see you!"

Ellie giggled as she saw them together. They looked so similar! If it weren't for the fact that Santa was a bit taller and much fatter, with a longer, curlier beard, it would have been difficult to tell them apart.

Summer pinched herself. She couldn't believe she was actually seeing the real-life Santa Claus!

Santa patted King Merry on the back, almost knocking him over. "What day is it?" he asked. "Have I missed Christmas?"

"Not yet," King Merry told him. "Today is Christmas Day!"

"Christmas Day?" echoed Santa. "Well then, I must give you your presents!"

CRACK!

Suddenly a loud thunderclap echoed through the air.

"Not so fast!" snapped a voice from the sky above.

Everyone looked up to see Queen Malice flying towards them on a midnight-black sleigh pulled by eight ugly Storm Sprites. She raised her thunderbolt staff over her head menacingly.

"Santa may be free," she called, "but no one will get a chance to enjoy Christmas – my magic will see to that!"

Jasmine couldn't bear how upset and frightened everyone looked. "Stop it!" she yelled at the wicked queen. "Go away!"

Queen Malice shrieked with glee. "Oh, I shall…" she called tauntingly, "but not before I've ruined Christmas – for good this time!" She shook her staff at the castle, and a green thunderbolt flew out of it and hit the castle wall with a big bang. Then, with a triumphant cackle, the queen sped away.

"What has she done now?" whispered Summer, searching the castle for any sign of change. "Everything looks the same as it was before."

Everyone looked very worried. Even Santa wasn't smiling. They rushed back into the castle to find out what Queen Malice had done.

As she walked through the door of the great hall, Ellie gasped.

"Oh, no!" cried Jasmine as she followed Ellie inside.

The hall was bare. Every single Christmas decoration had gone.

"Our presents!" wailed Trixi, who was hovering beside Ellie on her leaf. She pointed to a pile of dust sitting under the tree where the presents should have been.

"And look at the tree!" cried King

Merry. The beautiful Christmas tree was
nothing but bare branches. "She even
took the Shining Star!"

"Our stockings are gone too," said a
mermaid sadly.

Trixi burst into tears. All around them,

other pixies, imps, fairies, elves and brownies did the same.

"Queen Malice has ruined Christmas after all!" an imp said sadly.

"There isn't even anything to eat," Hailstone said, rubbing his belly hungrily.

Everyone sighed as they looked at the dining table. Where there had been a beautiful feast laid out just a little while earlier, there was now only dust.

"Christmas Day is nearly over anyway," one of the unicorns sniffed.

"Perhaps we should just give up and go home," King Merry suggested. "We can celebrate next year."

"Wait!" cried Ellie. "Christmas isn't ruined! Christmas isn't just about presents and food and a tree. It's about having fun together, and we can still do that. We can sing carols, dance and play games." She looked around hopefully at everyone.

"We can tell stories!" said Summer.

"But what about the feast?" a brownie cried out. "I'm starving!"

"Can you magic up more food?" Jasmine asked Trixi hopefully.

Trixi tapped her pixie ring, but it just sputtered miserably. "No," she said, shaking her tiny head. "Queen Malice's spell has taken all the magic away from Christmas Castle."

"But we can make some food in the kitchens!" one of the elves from the Sugarsweet Bakery said, rolling up his sleeves.

"The brownie band can play Christmas music," called Hailstone.

"And we mermaids can lead everyone

in some carols!" one of the mermaids chimed in.

Everyone started to talk excitedly.

"My goodness!" King Merry said, adjusting his glasses. "You girls are right. Of course we can still enjoy Christmas!"

"Ho, ho, ho!" Santa grinned. "Well, let's get started!"

Christmas Magic

Soon Christmas Castle was ringing with the sound of laughter. The brownies set up their instruments and started to play, while the elves from the Sugarsweet Bakery began working in the kitchen, making biscuits and hot chocolate. The delicious smell of baking gingerbread soon wafted through the hall. Jasmine, Summer and Ellie swept the nasty dust away into a corner while everyone else worked together to build a fire without their magic. The imps laid wood in the fireplace, the pixies gathered some wood chippings for kindling and then one of the unicorns lit the fire with a spark from her horn.

Santa's reindeer came in from the barn and lay by the fire while everyone else helped themselves to the mugs of hot chocolate topped with whipped cream and marshmallows that the elves had brought round. There were tiny mugs for the fairies and pixies, medium-sized mugs for the brownies and elves, and enormous mugs for Santa and King Merry, who were now sitting side by side in armchairs in front of the fireplace. Everything was starting to feel Christmassy again.

"Let's sing some carols!" said Summer.

"Can we sing '*Deck the Halls with*

Pixie Magic'?" asked Trixi. "That's my favourite."

The brownie band struck up a merry tune. The mermaids began to sing, their

beautiful voices ringing out around
the hall. When they got to the chorus,
everyone else joined in. Even the reindeer
stamped their hooves and waved their
antlers in time to the music.

Summer looked around the room and
smiled. She felt a burst of happiness filling
her when she saw how jolly everyone
looked as they sang together. When her
gaze fell on Santa, she gasped. He wasn't
just smiling – he was beaming from
ear to ear and sparkling all over with a
golden light!

Summer nudged Ellie and Jasmine.
They followed her gaze and broke off
from singing, their eyes widening.

"What's happening to Santa?"
whispered Jasmine.

"Ho, ho, ho," boomed Santa as he

glittered and shone. "Keep singing, my
friends!"

"But what's going on, Cousin?" cried
King Merry anxiously.

"It's magic!" Santa said.
"Your Christmas
cheer is
bringing the
magic back
to the
castle!"

The
brownies
played
even more
loudly and
everyone sang
extra joyfully for
the final chorus.

"Ho, ho, ho," chuckled Santa as they reached the last note.

The sparkling light coming from him now filled the room, rushing over the Christmas tree, the big empty dining table and the pile of dust in the corner. Everyone broke off from singing to gasp in amazement as the room transformed before their eyes. When the light finally faded out, the Christmas tree was alive with pine needles again and decorated with beautiful big silver and gold bows. The Shining Star shone brightly. The dining table was covered with a snowy-white tablecloth and filled with food: four enormous roast turkeys, great big tureens of crispy roast potatoes and peas, enormous jugs of gravy, heaping bowls of cranberry sauce, a huge flaming

Christmas pudding and a tray of fresh mince pies. And best of all, the dust had disappeared and the stockings hanging around the hearth had reappeared and were suddenly full of brightly wrapped presents!

"Merry Christmas, everyone!" boomed Santa.

"What…what's happened?" stammered Summer in amazement.

"It's very special
Christmas magic,"
said Santa,
looking around
at everyone's
astonished
faces. "You
made it
happen, all
of you. You
were right, girls.
Christmas isn't really
about presents and a tree. It's about being
together, sharing happy times, having
fun with your friends and families. And
because you remembered that, you made
the Christmas magic happen. Now, find
your presents, everyone, and then it's time
for us to eat!"

There was a massive cheer and everyone ran to get their stockings. Ellie, Summer and Jasmine stood together and watched as their friends all unwrapped their presents.

"Oh, look, a new hat!" cried Trixi, holding up a hat made out of delicate rose petals. "And my dress! The Storm Sprites didn't destroy it after all!"

"The snuggly slippers I wanted…and a new nightcap!" cried King Merry as he pulled the slippers and a long stripy nightcap out of some wrapping paper.

"Oh, isn't this wonderful?" said Summer. She loved seeing the delight on everyone's faces.

"It's completely brilliant!" declared Jasmine.

"And it's all thanks to you," Santa said, beaming at them. "Without your determination and courage, Christmas Day would not have been a very happy one this year in the Secret Kingdom. Thank you for rescuing me and helping everyone discover the real meaning of Christmas."

"You're very welcome," Summer said, blushing.

"Now, I have something for you," Santa said.

"But we've already opened our presents back in our world, Santa," said Ellie.

Santa's eyes twinkled. "Oh, it's just a little extra – a special gift to say thank you." He reached into the pocket of his red jacket and pulled out three beautiful glass ornaments. He handed one shaped like a reindeer to Summer, a dancing fairy to Jasmine and a pixie sitting on a leaf to Ellie. Each ornament hung from a rainbow-coloured ribbon and seemed to sparkle with its own magic light.

"Hang these on your trees at home and your Christmases will be sure to be extra magical every year," he said softly. "Look after them well."

"We will," breathed the girls. "Thank you!"

"And now, I think it's time you returned home for your own Christmas dinner, my dears," Santa said with a kind smile.

Summer nodded. Although the food on the dining table looked really delicious, she suddenly realised that she really wanted to have Christmas dinner with her own family – watching Connor refuse to eat his Brussels sprouts like he always did, and laughing as Finn made everyone wear the hats from their crackers. She wanted to see her mum smile and feel Mike give her a hug, and to be the one to read out all the silly jokes from the crackers. "Yes," she said softly. "I think it is time to go home."

Ellie and Jasmine nodded. Summer could tell they were thinking about their own families too.

"Trixi!" Santa called. The little pixie zoomed over on her leaf.

"Oh dear, is it really time for you to go?" she asked the girls.

"It is," said Ellie. "But we'd love to come back soon."

"Oh, I think you will," King Merry said, walking over to them. "Who knows what my sister will get up to next."

"If you need us, just send us a message in the Magic Box," said Jasmine. "We'll come straight away."

"We promise," Summer added.

King Merry looked at them for a moment and then smiled. "I don't know what we'd do without you three girls. That Magic Box really was one of my best inventions!"

Trixi nodded as she landed her leaf on his shoulder. "Goodbye for now!" she smiled.

"Goodbye, King Merry! Goodbye, Trixi! Goodbye, Santa!" called the girls as Trixi tapped her ring and a glittering light surrounded them. "And Happy Christmas, everyone!"

"Happy Christmas!" they heard all their friends in the Secret Kingdom cry, and then they were whisked away.

The girls landed back on the floor in Summer's room. For a moment they all blinked, trying to get used to being in Summer's bedroom and not the great hall at Christmas Castle.

Jasmine looked down at the glass fairy ornament in her hands. "Oh, wow," she

said, holding it up to the light and seeing that it still sparkled just as it had in the Secret Kingdom. "What an amazing adventure!"

"We actually got to meet Santa!" said Ellie.

"And help him," said Summer.

"Not just him, but all our friends," said Jasmine. "Though I'm quite glad we didn't eat at Christmas Castle. Imagine having two Christmas dinners!"

"Our tummies would be as big as Santa's by the end of the day!" giggled Ellie.

"This has been the best Christmas ever," Jasmine said happily.

"And it's not over yet," Ellie reminded her. "We've got the rest of Christmas Day to celebrate here."

Summer hid the
Magic Box
underneath
her little
Christmas
tree, and
then
carefully
hung her
reindeer
ornament
on the topmost
branch. The reindeer's
nose glowed red for a second and then
the colour faded away. "I hope we do go
back to the Secret Kingdom soon," she
said.

Jasmine nodded. "For more adventures,"
she added happily.

"And lots more fun!" said Ellie.

Summer glanced at the Magic Box under the tree. A message would appear in it again one day – she was sure of it. "Merry Christmas, Secret Kingdom," she whispered. "See you soon."

**In the next Secret Kingdom
adventure, Ellie, Summer and
Jasmine visit**

Bubble Volcano

Read on for a sneak peek...

A Special Invitation

"Summer, come on!" Jasmine Smith
urged. "Ellie will be wondering where we
are!"

"Just a minute!" Summer Hammond
was crouched on the ground, her blonde
pigtails falling over her shoulders as
she coaxed a tiny red ladybird off the
pavement and onto her hand. She gently
placed it down on a nearby wall. "It'll be

safe there," she said to Jasmine. "I couldn't leave it. Someone might have trodden on it."

Jasmine smiled. Summer loved all animals, even insects like ladybirds. "When you're older, you'll have to get a job on one of those TV animal shows where they film at a zoo or a vet's office."

Summer looked horrified. "Oh, no. I'd hate to be on TV."

"I'd love it!" said Jasmine. She flung her arms out and twirled round. Her long dark hair flew around her shoulders as she spun. "Imagine being an actress, or even better, a pop star!"

Summer grinned. She and Jasmine and their other best friend, Ellie Macdonald, were all very different from one another, but maybe that was why they all got on so well – that, and the fact they shared an amazing magical secret, of course! Summer felt a tingle of excitement run through her as she thought about the precious object inside her bag.

"Come on, slowcoach!" she teased Jasmine. "I'll race you to Ellie's!"

"You're here!" Ellie squealed, flinging open the door as Jasmine and Summer ran up the drive, panting and out of breath. The three girls hugged. Ellie had been on holiday for two whole weeks. Her usually pale skin was covered with freckles from the sun and her red curls were slightly lighter. "Come in!" she cried as she dragged Jasmine and Summer inside.

"Hi, girls!" Mrs Macdonald called from the kitchen.

Jasmine and Summer chorused hello.

"We're going to my room, Mum!" Ellie called.

The girls bounded upstairs to Ellie's bedroom. Jasmine looked around at the purple walls, which were covered with pictures that Ellie had drawn herself. It felt like ages since she had last been here – two weeks was a long time to be apart from one of your best friends!

"Ta-da!" Ellie cried as she picked two little presents up off the desk and held them out to Jasmine and Summer. They were wrapped in paper she had decorated herself. She had drawn rabbits on Summer's and musical notes on Jasmine's. "These are for you. I bought them in Spain."

"Oh, thank you!" Jasmine and Summer

exclaimed, quickly unwrapping the gifts. Inside Jasmine's was a small model of a dark-haired flamenco dancer wearing a red silk dress and inside Summer's there was a toy donkey with long ears and a very cute face.

"Thanks, Ellie!" Jasmine smiled. "I love it!"

"My donkey's so sweet!" said Summer, stroking its furry head.

Ellie beamed. "I'm glad you like them." She lowered her voice. "So what's been going on here while I've been away? You didn't go you-know-where without me, did you?" she asked anxiously.

"No!" Jasmine grinned. "We haven't had any messages in the you-know-what."

"You mean this you-know-what?"

Summer asked, pulling a wooden box out of her bag.

"The Magic Box!" breathed Ellie.

Summer put it down on the rug gently. It had mermaids, unicorns and other wonderful creatures carved into its sides, and in the middle of its lid there was a mirror surrounded by six green gems.

The Magic Box came from a place called the Secret Kingdom. King Merry, the ruler there, had made it to help save the kingdom. When he was chosen to lead instead of his nasty sister, Queen Malice, the evil queen had hidden six horrible thunderbolts around the Secret Kingdom to cause problems and ruin everyone's fun. The Magic Box had travelled to the human world and found the only people who could break Queen Malice's awful spells – Summer, Jasmine and Ellie!

With the help of King Merry's pixie assistant, Trixi, and lots of wonderful friends from the Secret Kingdom, the girls had broken all six of Malice's thunderbolts and helped the enchanted land return to peace and happiness. Queen Malice had sworn that she would find another way to rule the Secret Kingdom, but so far there were no more signs of trouble.

"It's been ages since we got any messages in the Magic Box," said Jasmine. "Nothing's happened for months!"

"That's probably good – for the Secret Kingdom, anyway," pointed out Summer. "It must mean everything is fine there."

Jasmine sighed. "I don't want anything bad to happen in the Secret Kingdom, but I really wish we could visit again!"

"Or at least open the Magic Box!" Ellie cried. "If we could see all the amazing gifts we've been given, then it wouldn't feel so much like we dreamed it all!"

Read
Bubble Volcano
to find out what happens next!

Secret Kingdom

Look out for the next sparkling series!

Bubble Volcano

ROSIE BANKS

Sugarsweet Bakery

ROSIE BANKS

Dream Dale

ROSIE BANKS

Lily Pad Lake

ROSIE BANKS

Midnight Maze

ROSIE BANKS

Fairytale Forest

ROSIE BANKS

Available
February 2013

Secret Kingdom

A magical world of friendship and fun!

Join best friends
Ellie, Summer and Jasmine at

www.secretkingdombooks.com

and enjoy games, sneak peeks
and lots more!

You'll find great activities, competitions, stories
and games, plus a special newsletter for
Secret Kingdom friends!

Secret Kingdom

Would you like to win a Secret Kingdom goodie bag?

All you have to do is copy this picture of Christmas Castle and draw you and your best friend there!

We will put all of your wonderful pictures into a draw and one lucky winner will win a fabulous goodie bag of sparkly treats!

Send your entry to Secret Kingdom Christmas Castle Drawing Competition, Orchard Books, 338 Euston Road, London, NW1 3BH
There will be two prize draws which will take place on the 30th April 2013 and 31st July 2013.
Competition open only to UK and Republic of Ireland residents.
No purchase necessary.
For full terms and conditions please go to www.secretkingdombooks.com